Wacky Waddles

Written by Miranda Hardy   Illustrated by Rimi Rasheed

Wacky Waddles is a work of fiction. All characters and events presented within these pages are a product of the author's imagination. Any resemblance to actual events, locales, organizations, or persons, living or dead, is entirely coincidental.

Published by

Quixotic Publishing LLC
P.O. Box 1311
Boynton Beach, FL 33474-1311
Website: www.quixoticpublishing.com

ISBN: 978-1-939588-00-5

Text copyright © 2013 Miranda Hardy
Cover and illustrations copyright © 2013 Rimi Rasheed

To Faith & Cody,
~M.H~

To Hud & Insha with love,
~R.R~

Wacky Waddles was new to the zoo.
Where should he go? What should he do?

Wacky Waddles tried to balance on one leg like the flamingo, but when they talked, he couldn't understand their lingo.

The ostrich liked to hide, and Wacky Waddles decided to try.

Wacky Waddles realized he didn't like the grit, and he turned his head to spit.

The penguins looked happy sliding on the ice, but Wacky Waddles didn't think it felt very nice.

Peacocks soon came into view and their wings spread and grew.

Waddles stretched like a superstar ...

but he didn't get very far.

Beautiful parrots perched on branches nearby.
Their colors shone brightly beneath the sky.

Wacky Waddles tried to paint his feathers
blue and green, but the colors faded
and lost their sheen.

During the day the bats would sleep,
hanging in a tree above the sheep.

Wacky Waddles tried to hang upside down. Soon his smile turned to a frown, and he landed on his crown.

A rooster crowed, "cock-a-doodle-do," and Wacky Waddles blew and blew.

But he blew so hard and fell back.
All that came out was,

The pelicans gulped down their fish but that wasn't Wacky's favorite dish.

Wacky Waddles felt like a chump and wanted to curl up in a big lump. When a wise ole owl swooped down and began to look around.

" You seem so distraught, Why do you try to be what you're not?"

"All of the others can do wonderful things and all I have is a dull pair of wings."

"Young Wacky Waddles, you do not see. You are special, you have to agree. You will be liked for who you are. You will learn to go very far. Cheer up and go on your way, and remember to always have a good day."

Wacky Waddles found what he was searching for, loving friends and so much more.

ACKNOWLEDGMENT

I'd like to thank so many extraordinary people for being a part of this fabulous journey. To my family, who supports my wacky ways. To Rimi, who shines brightly on the inside and out. To Ainsley Shay, my accomplice, my editor, my friend ... I couldn't have accomplished this without you. To Gwen Gardner, who was instrumental in helping to release Wacky Waddles into the world. To my blogging friends, whose help and encouragement pushed me along. And, most of all, to my readers. Wacky Waddles appreciates you!

~Miranda Hardy~

To my dear husband, thank you for always believing in me and encouraging me to follow my passion. I could not have done this without your constant support. Very special thanks to Miranda, who started it all and made this book a joy to work on, that I am truly proud of. Not to forget, to my family and to all Wacky Waddles readers', I hope you all enjoy reading this as much as I enjoyed illustrating it. Thank you!

~Rimi Rasheed~

ABOUT THE AUTHOR

Miranda Hardy writes children's literature to keep the voices in her head appeased. When she's not in her fantasy world, she's canoeing in alligator infested waters, or rescuing homeless animals. She resides in south Florida with her two wonderful children, and too many animals to mention.

ABOUT THE ILLUSTRATOR

Rimi Rasheed is a professional in primary education yet follows a passion in digital illustrating, and much of her work is focused on children. She is well known for her colourful creations of lovable characters, most of which can be found on her blog, www.doodleisle.com. She lives in Maldives with her husband and two children.